Pat Hutchins

WHICH WITCH IS WHICH?

Julia MacRae Books

A DIVISION OF WALKER BOOKS

Copyright © 1989 Pat Hutchins
All rights reserved
First published in the USA 1989
by Greenwillow Books
First published in Great Britain 1990
by Julia MacRae Books
A division of Walker Books Ltd
87 Vauxhall Walk
London SE11 5HJ

Printed and bound by Imago in Hong Kong

British Library Cataloguing in Publication Data
Hutchins, Pat, 1942–
Which witch is which?
I. Title
823'.914 [J]

ISBN 0-86203-430-2

Ella and Emily looked the same,
and were often called
by each other's name.
Ella likes pink, Emily blue.

Which witch is which?

They played tug of war,
three on each side,

and Mouse's mother had to decide
if Ella or Emily's team had won.

Which witch is which?

They all had an ice cream
before the next game.
Cowboy chose strawberry,
Ella the same.

The rest had vanilla
with chocolate chips.

Which witch is which?

They played musical chairs
and skipped and hopped

until one chair was left
and the music stopped.

One witch on the chair,
one witch on the floor.

Which witch is which?

After musical chairs
it was time for tea,

and Mouse's mother
brought in the cake.
Ella had cake,
Emily did not.

Which witch is which?

At six o'clock
they chose a balloon,
as their parents would be
collecting them soon.

Ella chose pink,
Emily blue.

Which witch is which?